Whiskers

and the

Pieces of Eight

Whiskers
and the
Pieces of Eight

Story plundered from
Pauline Mackay

Booty-fully illustrated by
Dylan Gibson

Ablekids   Press

Published in Scotland in 2014 by
Ablekids Press Ltd,
46 Ballifeary Road, Inverness, IV3 5PF

1 3 5 7 9 10 8 6 4 2

www.ablekidspress.com

ISBN: 978-1-910280-08-9

Printed in Scotland by Bell & Bain Ltd
Typeset by Raspberry Creative Type

A CIP catalogue record for this book is available from the British Library

To Cait, whose wonderful enthusiasm brought
this story into existence and who is herself,
without doubt, a treasure.

Ahoy, matey!

My parents were immigrants who left home
to live and work in London. This was hard for
our family. Sometimes we felt lost and alone,
far from all the things which told the story
of who we were and where we came from –
landscape, art, music, history and language.

To make us feel better, we went looking
for new stories. Often, we went to museums.
I remember my first one, the Victoria and
Albert – a palace of the past. As a child of 'lost
place parents', I still recall the feeling I had
when I stepped into its galleries. I looked at all
the delights: every case, every exhibit, and I
gasped: 'This is all mine!' And it *was*.

Today, I am lucky enough to work in a
museum. I have the chance to share my 'first
museum' excitement with visitors; to see their
faces as they step into an incredible adventure;
to guide them round a walk-in treasure chest.
Treasure! Does that mean pirate's gold?

Museums collect all sorts of items. Some are priceless. Many of these precious treasures have grown valuable over time. Perhaps no other example remains in existence or their value lies in helping us understand how people once lived.

Some examples of the objects, specimens and archives that can be found in a museum are: jewellery and coins; preserved animals (taxidermy), some of which may now be extinct; fossils of long-dead species, such as dinosaurs; paintings and books; weapons and tools.

So remember, when you visit a museum, you are answering a special invitation to discover its treasures and to understand their real value and importance. And don't forget that we share this treasure – our knowledge about the past, stories of people's lives and information about the natural world. It is all ours!

Cait McCullagh
Curator – Collections Engagement
Inverness Museum

Chapter 1

One misty morning in September, a damp little package arrived at Inverness Museum, addressed rather mysteriously

'To anyone who cares'.

It landed on Kate the Curator's desk, only to be buried immediately under a pile of newly delivered letters, while she was showing a group of schoolchildren some of the museum's treasures: Pictish

stones, fossils, Viking and Jacobite artefacts.

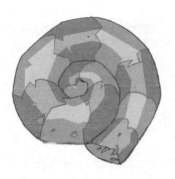

'Treasure' was a word visitors heard often from Kate as she sailed effortlessly back in time, bringing the rich history of the area to life.

Adults were encouraged to handle precious exhibits to help them connect with the past. Children, too, were held captive by the unusual, ancient objects placed in their hands.

4

When she eventually returned to her desk, Kate was struck by the odd arrangement of the unopened letters awaiting her attention. They were lying in the shape of an

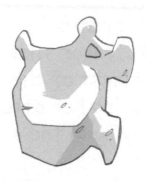

Chapter 2

That evening, out of nowhere, a
sea breeze blew slowly through the
museum, lingering in some spots as
if it had special business there.

The whole building creaked and groaned as if it was reluctantly coming to life.

Suddenly, Whiskers, a rather fine specimen of a black water vole from the Fresh Water display, found himself running along the floor of the museum.

A small object came bouncing straight into him, making him squeak with surprise.

It turned out to be a very old, worn coin, but there was something else, too. Faint fingerprints swirled on either side of the dull metal, as if, long ago, someone had been holding on so tightly that their mark was left forever.

An unexpected growl broke the salty silence.

"Shiver me timbers! That scurvy piece o' silver has grown legs. See if you can find it, Talons."

Whiskers jumped at the sound of the gravelly voice, barely managing to stop another squeak. Most importantly for the little water vole, who was Talons? With a name like that, it couldn't be good!

Just as Whiskers' long hairy tail slipped out of sight behind a stone basin, which was standing nearby, he got his answer and froze in fear.

A tawny owl swooped down, grabbed the coin in its deadly talons and flew away over the display cases.

When Whiskers regained the use of his legs, he bravely decided to head in the same direction, in the hope of understanding what was going on and why he was in this strange place.

An old, bearded man, dressed in oilskins, was sitting by a yellowing piece of whale bone, mending sails.

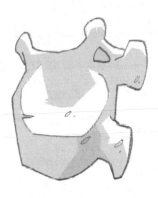

As he worked, he swayed from side to side, singing the following shanty:

A single drop o' pirate blood
Flowed deep through th' veins o' Kate
That precious drop wer just enough
For th' pirate piece o' eight.

On Longship Island's 'idden cove
For th' centuries four or five
That plunder'd coin lay awaitin'
Pirate blood, to come alive.

Th' finder 'ad no buccaneers
In 'is family long ago
'e 'id 'is booty wrapped in silk
Tied up wi' a velvet bow.

'is widow later found this prize
And thought some jewel to see;
'er anger sent th' museum
A borin', old coin for free.

When that peice o' pirate silver
Sat 'n Kate's ancestral 'and
'er pirate blood turned mutinous
n' her feet grew tired o' land.

Eight days transformin' from 'ersel'
To a swagg'rin' Cap'n Kate,
Eight items she must gather up
Then at last 'twill be too late.

'er ghostly ship'll fast appear
And strip the museum bare,
All yer treaures gone forever
To th' Cap'n's pirate lair!

Whiskers couldn't believe his ears. How could anyone who worked at the museum be turning into a horrible pirate? It was too ridiculous!

Just at that moment, Kate staggered round a huge display case, wearing a skull and crossbones bandana.

"Don't worry, me hearties," she cried. "Thar'll be a fair wind blowin' before long 'n then we'll be able to make shore. This storm's like a bellyache after too much rich grub. It'll soon pass."

Talons, perhaps wisely, chose to perch on a dried-out display branch, rather than risk a bumpy ride on Kate's shoulder!

"Cap'n Kate'll soon 'ave her sea legs," laughed the old man confidently, as she lurched round another corner and disappeared.

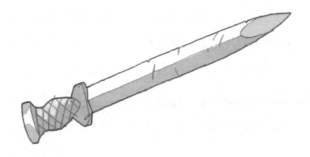

Chapter 3

For the next two days, the museum was closed and absolutely still, apart from Whiskers exploring this new, completely alien territory. His search for a river, stream or pool was in vain.

The only other creatures were all motionless, with glassy, unseeing eyes. Among them, in one of the woodland displays, was a tawny owl which looked exactly like Talons.

As for the old man mending sails in the painting which hung on one of the museum's walls, he wasn't real!

By Monday night, Whiskers might have convinced himself it was all a bad dream, if it wasn't for the fact he just couldn't explain his own presence in the museum!

On Tuesday morning Kate breezed into work.

"Ahoy, me hearties!" were her first words to the other staff. Saturday's skull and crossbones bandana was twisted loosely round her neck. A large, gold hoop earring dangled boldly from her right ear, and a smudged pirate ship tattoo bobbed in and out of sight on the pale skin of her left upper arm.

A few hours later, Whiskers looked on aghast as a jagged, weather-worn piece of oak, salvaged by Kate from an unknown source, was hoisted above the door of the Discovery Room. On it was scrawled: Captain Kate's Cabin.

That night, an oil lamp flickered in the Discovery Room, revealing its

transformation into a ship's cabin, fit for an ambitious pirate captain.

Kate sat, eerie shadows dancing around her, plotting with her increasingly sinister accomplice.

Whiskers remembered the shanty.

What were the eight things Kate had to gather? Despite the terrifying silhouette of Talons clamped to a chair in a dark corner of the Cabin, Whiskers hid by the open door and listened.

"Aye, 'tis a fine piece of oak, indeed, Cap'n. It's got th' pedigree to bring back an ocean-skimmin', wind-lovin' schooner 'n ah'll 'ave all th' sails ye'll be needin' mended by Friday."

"See they are, Needles or ye'll be the first one greetin' th' keel o' my ship!" Kate's eyes narrowed

and she rubbed her gold earring.
Her sea sickness would be gone
by Saturday. "Everythin' 'll be
gone by Saturday!" she roared out
triumphantly, extinguishing the
lamp.

Whiskers couldn't sleep a wink.
Kate was behaving very oddly, yet
no-one in the museum seemed to
be worried. How could he save Kate
and the museum from impending
pirate doom?

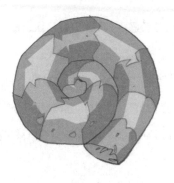

Chapter 4

Bleary-eyed and nervous as the sun rose, Whiskers dreaded what would unfold that day. The fragment of conversation he had overheard the night before certainly made it clear that Saturday was the fateful day, and, judging from Kate's confidence, the eight pieces of the pirate puzzle were falling easily into place. Whiskers had nothing more to go on, while

Needles, quiet and calm in his picture again, knew everything!

On Wednesday afternoon, Kate headed for the Cabin, a large, bulging canvas bag slung over her shoulder. Whiskers noted her stagger had already disappeared, replaced by what could only be described as the hint of a swagger.

The silver piece of eight, which had bounced into him several days earlier, was hanging round Kate's neck. The fingerprints, so faint before, now furrowed deeply into the silver, as if someone's life depended, once more, on holding on to it.

Kate unfurled a huge banner.

International Talk like a Pirate Day!

The museum was preparing for a family day of pirate fun. Kate was only doing her job – incredibly enthusiastically. Needles? He was obviously part of the show.

That night, one very tired and relieved little water vole slept peacefully, unaware of an important meeting between Kate and Needles.

Curled up and well hidden in a
warm, cosy corner, he also missed
Talons flying frantically around the
displays. The tawny owl was hunting
for Whiskers!

On Thursday, Kate indulged in a jig or two as she went about her day's work. This made the coins in a silky pouch, hanging from her thick leather belt, jingle and jangle, putting a big smile on her face.

"Better mind me treasure!" Whiskers heard her say loudly to laughing visitors several times.

Some of them said they'd be attending the family fun day. That made her smile even more, and twist the thick gold ring which had appeared on her thumb.

"Splendid, me hearties. By th' end o' th' day, ye'll all be real pirates, for sure!"

When Whiskers poked his nose into the Cabin that evening, he saw a Jolly Roger raised above the banner.

"A pirate flag for the pirate ship?" he wondered, then gave himself a shake.

Out by the whale bone, Needles was hard at work. Perhaps it was intuition, but Whiskers scurried under a fold of sail just in time. Talons came to rest on the dried branch above Needles' head and listened intently, but any giveaway noises were drowned out by the old man bursting into the shanty which had so alarmed Whiskers.

"Call me blood mutinous again 'n ah'll make sure ye dine on weevils for a month, ye dirty bilge rat!" threatened Kate as she sprung out unexpectedly in front of Needles.

Talons settled on her shoulder and fixed him with an unnerving stare.

"Blisterin' barnacles, Cap'n. Ne'er meant no 'arm by it. Just a way o' sayin' what quality pirate blood ye've got!"

"Look lively, ye old sea dog and turn these silver groats into 'lucky' pieces o' eight!"

From his hiding place, Whiskers heard the coins being rattled impatiently.

"That be up to yersel', Cap'n, not a scurvy dog like me. Hold yer pirate piece o' eight tight, then dip it into that thar old pouch, made from silk that touched the skin o' Cap'n Kidd!"

"Arrrrrrgh," crowed Kate, pleased with the result.

"Tomorrow, we'll gather up th' pistols, cutlasses and a sweet, silver timepiece. Ah can taste that salty sea air already 'n Talons here'll earn 'er keep better than any parrot."

Whiskers' sleek, black fur stood on end. Something *really* was wrong.

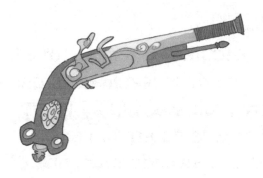

Chapter 5

The first unwelcome sound on Friday wasn't the jingle, jangle of unnatural coins. It was a tinkling of keys. Someone was opening the display cases. That someone, of course had to be ... no, it couldn't be ...

NEEDLES!

Dressed like a member of staff, the bunch of museum keys dangling merrily from his sinewy wrist, Needles was about to remove pistols and swords from one of the cases when Mary, a museum employee, rushed up.

"Stop! Stop! What are you doing?"

Whiskers gulped as Needles turned slowly.

"You forgot the cotton gloves. You must wear these when touching certain exhibits. I know it's your first day here at the museum. There's a lot to learn. Let me help you move these to the Cabin."

Needles gave a cold, hard smile and put on the gloves.

Anxious not to believe what he was seeing with his own eyes, Whiskers rushed to check on the painting of Kate's co-conspirator.

It had gone!

Talons, however, sat rigidly on display, her eyes dark and empty.

Later, Whiskers watched Needles brazenly help himself to an elegant silver watch from the

Jacobite collection. He added it, with great satisfaction, to the growing pile of pistols and swords – which Kate had taken to calling cutlasses.

Everything she had listed was gathered in one place. Yet as the museum shut for the night, Whiskers was no closer to making sense of what was happening and time was most definitely running out!

In light of the good fortune which they felt sure was about to shine on them, Kate and Needles spent the evening in the Cabin, laughing and toasting the stupidity of landlubbers.

Needles' staff uniform had been abandoned in favour of an ill-fitting cotton shirt, threadbare waistcoat and torn breeches, topped off by

a gaudy red bandana tied tightly round his straggly grey hair. The soles of his feet were like dried-out strips of old leather. An ugly scar sliced through the brown, creased skin of his left cheek and two gold teeth glinted every time he roared with laughter at the Captain's jokes.

Kate's appearance was no less astonishing. A white, silk blouse flounced from beneath a crimson, damask waistcoat while a black belt, studded with gold, swept round billowing velvet breeches. Bucket boots, polished and gleaming, adorned her feet. On her head, a plain broad-brimmed hat boasted a band of golden ribbon and three magnificent peacock feathers, which flapped gently like sails waiting for a fair wind.

As the wick on the oil lamp
burned low, Needles left the
Cabin with Talons who was
determined on one last hunt. The
disappearance of the water vole
was an irritating mistake which
Kate had successfully explained
away to staff. Talons' inability to
catch it had angered her more. As
the heavy doors of the Discovery
Room swung slowly shut behind

them, Whiskers, in a moment of desperation, darted inside.

Kate yawned and stretched, ready to leave too, but then slumped over the table. Exhausted by the adventures of the past week and the excitement of what was still to come, she fell instantly asleep. And that was when Whiskers finally discovered what lay in store the following day!

Chapter 6

At first, all remained quiet in the Cabin except for the faintest crackle of the burning lamp wick. Needles had left a piece of sail cloth draped over a chair. Whiskers climbed up it and jumped onto the table. The peacock feathers now hovered like three unblinking eyes.

Lying on the table was the pouch of coins which seemed to be a very important part of Kate's plan.

Whiskers loosened the drawstring and gently dragged one of the coins into view. It certainly wasn't a groat from the museum's display. It was a silver Spanish dollar – a piece of eight – like the one round Kate's neck.

"Ah'll teach those landlubbers a thing or two!" mumbled Kate suddenly, grasping the pouch. The coin Whiskers had been examining dropped with a plop onto the table. Cowering beside the pouch, too terrified to clamber back down the sail, he realised Kate was still asleep. However, she kept talking.

"Timber 'n sails for a sturdy, seaworthy ship; pistols 'n cutlasses to fight a good fight; a gold ring for treasure; a watch to turn back time to th' good old days; 'n pirate pieces o' eight to buy Cap'n Kate ... aaarrrgh ..."

A deep rumble of a laugh rolled from her lips; her eyelids flickered but remained closed. Whiskers gave a huge shiver and his tail

accidentally swiped the pouch.
The coins inside ground together,
coaxing Kate to reveal the eighth
and final item she needed to bring
her plan to life -

"'n pirate pieces o' eight to buy
Cap'n Kate ... an unsuspectin' crew!"

Whiskers finally understood.

International Talk like a Pirate Day was a clever trap. Families were going to turn up on Saturday expecting fun activities, but the only activity of interest to Kate would be getting them to accept her 'special' pirate coins, which would transform them into a cut-throat pirate crew.

"By th' end o' th' day, ye'll all be real pirates, for sure!"

That's what she had repeated over and over again when people said they were coming along.

Her ghostly pirate ship might have some crew straight from Davy Jones' Locker, but flesh-and-blood Kate needed some flesh-and-blood crew. With a ship at her command, the museum would be plundered of its treasures!

How could Captain Kate be outwitted? Getting rid of the coins seemed like a good idea. Whiskers was pushing the first one towards the edge of the table, ready to slide it silently down the sail cloth, when he stopped.

Kate would just turn other old coins into pieces of eight as soon as she discovered they were missing.

As he tried to roll the coin back to the pouch, Kate thumped the table, still caught up in her pirate dream. Whiskers lost his grip and watched in horror as the coin took off in the direction of her mouth, which was opening in a large, noisy snore!

At the last second, it wobbled and fell against the piece of eight tied round Kate's neck, which was jutting out from under her chin. Something totally unexpected happened!

The coin returned to its original form – a groat.

This gave Whiskers a tiny hope. What if he changed all the coins back to groats? Would Kate think to check them before handing them out to the families tomorrow?

Whiskers worked very hard that night, dragging every dangerous piece of eight from the pouch and refilling it with safe silver groats.

The fear that Kate might wake at any moment made his little heart race, but thankfully she slept soundly, unaware of any threat to her life of piracy.

Chapter 7

By the time Kate stirred early on Saturday morning, Whiskers had finished his task and found a hiding place behind the bag of presents ready to give out as prizes.

Stiff and annoyed at herself, Kate plucked the pouch from the table without a second glance, secured it to her belt and hurried off to fetch the wooden chest she had bought for her new home.

At 10.45a.m., Kate and Needles, both in full pirate attire, were standing at the door of Captain Kate's Cabin, welcoming families to the museum event.

Everyone had made an effort to dress like a pirate. Kate beamed as family after family arrived. Needles' rather fierce pirate look had parents and children chuckling with delight. His humourless grimaces as they pointed and complimented him on his realistic-looking scar made them hoot with laughter.

There was no hooting from Talons, who sat inside the Cabin tied securely to a perch. Kate explained that the owl was standing in for a parrot. Again, everyone thought this was terribly funny, while Talons eyed them coldly.

Much to Needles' annoyance, Kate insisted on entertaining her victims for a while. Perhaps this was just the last vestige of the old

Kate trying to hold on, or was she playing cruelly with them, like a cat with a mouse?

"Let's turn back time," she suggested, theatrically producing the silver timepiece and moving its hands backwards.

Whiskers could scarcely bear to watch. Kate explained how Vikings could be considered pirates, talked about a pox of piracy in the Western Isles, including around

Longship Island, and finished off with the infamous Scottish pirate, Captain William Kidd, who suffered a gruesome end.

With every mention of his name, Kate jingled the coins in her pouch.

"Well, me landlubbing good-for-nothings, time to make real pirates o' ye all," Kate finally announced.

Needles and Talons perked up.

"A treasure hunt is just what ye need to get yer pirate blood flowin'. Try out yer plunderin' 'ands in Needles' sack o' booty and get yer pirate silver 'ere. Then, we'll be off."

Kate shook the pouch. The coins hidden inside held a secret, but whose secret? Kate's or Whiskers'?

Needles lunged forward and grabbed the bag of prizes, catapulting Whiskers right under Talons' nose. Shackled to the perch, the tawny owl flapped up and down, desperately trying to break free.

"Stop that noise, ye scabby pile o' feathers or ah'll be 'avin' ye stewed for me dinner!" yelled Kate.

Talons was quiet. Whiskers took refuge behind a corner of Needles' sail cloth. Parents grinned, thinking it was part of the show. The children squealed with laughter, jostling for their prizes and pirate silver. Parents distracted Kate with chatter. A flash of silver between tiny fingers was enough to convince her all was well.

As the last child skipped away clutching her 'treasure', a fierce look flitted across Kate's eyes. Whiskers could feel a slight breeze rising and the air in the room tasted strange.

A ghostly ship shimmered before them, just as Needles' shanty had predicted!

"Landlubbers, aboard!" ordered Captain Kate. "Swab the decks, hoist the sails. Any mutinous talk and ye'll walk th' plank at dawn, ye scurvy scallywags!"

A Jacob's ladder tumbled down for Captain Kate's crew … but no-one moved.

"Look smart, ye pustulant pilferers!"

Still no-one moved. Kate turned to Needles for help. He was gone. A gust of salty air whistled sharply through the room, taking the ship, and Kate's new life of piracy, with it.

"Awesome!" gasped the children and a round of applause rippled through the amazed parents.

As 'un-pirated' Kate led the group round the museum on a 'kind of treasure hunt', everyone recognised a hoard of silver groats lying in a display case.

"That's like our pirate silver!"

Kate couldn't believe her eyes.

"Ah think ye'll find yer treasure's been plundered, ye luckless layabouts!" wheezed a voice that sounded like Needles'.

All the old groats, handed out in Captain Kate's Cabin, lay back in their original case. While, in their place, to the delight of the children, were rather delicious chocolate coins!

"Can we be scurvy scallywags again next year, please?" asked one little boy.

Kate sighed. "Maybe we'll do something a little different next time."

As Whiskers felt himself drawn back to his waterside companions, he passed the woodland display. The tawny owl stood on the tree branch, its head tilted downwards.

A visitor left convinced she had seen the owl's talons tighten.

"Just a trick of the light, madam," Kate assured her. "The museum has been playing tricks on all of us today!"

Treasure Trove of Words
for Scurvy Scallywags

accomplice – someone who helps another person do bad things

ancestral – inherited from family members who lived in the past

archive – information kept about something

artefact – something made by people, especially an object of historical interest

attire – clothes

barnacle – small creature living in a shell which can attach itself to the bottom of a ship

bilge – lowest area of a ship below the waterline

breeches – trousers to the knee

buccaneer – pirate

bucket boots – knee-high, leather boots with a flared, bucket-shaped top

Captain William Kidd – probably the most famous Scottish pirate, born in Dundee in 1645; tried and executed for piracy in 1701

cowering – pulling back in fear

crimson – deep red colour

curator – administrative director of a museum or library

damask – expensive patterned fabric

extinct – has died out; no living form exists

fossil – something from a long time ago in the past, e.g. a footprint left in the ground or a dinosaur skeleton

furrowed – having deep, narrow grooves

groat – a silver coin used in Britain from the 14th to the 17th century

impending – going to happen soon

infamous – famous for being bad

intuition – knowing something without obvious clues

Jacobites – supporters of King James II and his family, who fought to restore the Stuarts to the British throne

Jacob's ladder – rope or chain ladder with wooden or metal rungs used on ships

keel – part of ship running from bow to stern below the centre of the hull

Longship Island – Longay (meaning Longship Island) lies off the Isle of Skye. The Western Isles of Scotland were full of pirates in the 16th and 17th centuries

oilskins – waterproof clothing

pedigree – a record of family stretching back generations

Pictish stones – large carved stones made by Picts, people who lived north of the Forth Estuary (6th to 9th century) in a part of Scotland then known as Pictland

piece of eight – a silver Spanish dollar

pilferer – thief

pox – disease

salvaged – saved from destruction (often used about ships)

schooner – type of ship typically with two masts

shanty – a song sung by sailors as they work

silhouette – outline of something filled in black

specimen – an example of something

timepiece – an instrument, like a pocket watch, which shows the time

vestige – very small amount

Vikings – Scandinavian sailors who raided the Highlands of Scotland in the 8th century

weevil – type of beetle which was common in dry food stored on ships, in the days before fridges and tins

Needles' Shanty

A single drop o' pirate blood
Flowed deep through th' veins o' Kate;
That precious drop wer just enough
For th' pirate piece o' eight.

On Longship Island's 'idden cove
For th' centuries four or five
That plunder'd coin lay awaitin'
Pirate blood, to come alive.

Th' finder 'ad no buccaneers
In 'is family long ago.
'e 'id 'is booty wrapped in silk
Tied up wi' a velvet bow.

'is widow later found this prize
And thought some jewel to see;
'er anger sent th' museum
A borin', old coin for free.

When that piece o' pirate silver,
Sat 'n Kate's ancestral 'and,
'er pirate blood turned mutinous
'n her feet grew tired o' land.

Eight days transformin' from 'ersel'
To a swagg'rin' Cap'n Kate,
Eight items she must gather up
Then at last 'twill be too late!

'er ghostly ship'll fast appear
And strip th' Museum bare,
All yer treasures gone forever
To th' Cap'n's pirate lair!

Born in Inverness, Scotland, Pauline Mackay has written several stories for young children. She is best known for her 'Wee MacNessie' picture books which are published in English and bilingual editions by Ablekids Press. Whether any pirate blood flows through her veins is unclear but guard your treasure, just in case!

Dylan Gibson be an illustrator
o' many things, includin' books
for sprogs.

When not drawin', he be spotted
out and about with his trusty
spaniel or cookin' up some treats in
th' kitchen.

Check out his other Ablekids Press
title 'The Fox and
the Grapes'.

Other titles from Ablekids Press

Picture books

Fruit Lane

Ceum Nam Measan

Mrs Blackberry's Tiring Day

Wee MacNessie

Where is Wee MacNessie?

The Fox and the Grapes

For more information on these titles,
including languages available,
please go to:
www.ablekidspress.com

Do you have a drop o' pirate blood flowin' through yer veins?